June Factor's other books for children include

Far Out, Brussel Sprout!

All Right, Vegemite!

Unreal, Banana Peel!

Real Keen, Baked Bean!

Ladles and Jellyspoons

Roll Over Pavlova!

Okey Dokey Karaoke!

Summer

Kidspeak: A Dictionary of Australian Children's Words, Expressions and Games

Child's Play: Dorothy Howard and the Folklore of Australian Children (co-edited with Kate Darian-Smith)

LOLs

Best Jokes for Kids

JUNE FACTOR

ILLUSTRATED BY MIC LOOBY

ALLEN&UNWIN

SYDNEY · MELBOURNE · AUCKLAND · LONDON

This edition first published in 2012

First published in 2000 as *June Factor's Juicy Jumping Joke Book*

Allen & Unwin
83 Alexander Street
Crows Nest NSW 2065
Australia
Phone: (61 2) 8425 0100
Fax: (61 2) 9906 2218
Email: info@allenandunwin.com
Web: www.allenandunwin.com

A Cataloguing-in-Publication entry is available from the National Library of Australia
www.trove.nla.gov.au

ISBN 978 1 74331 256 8

Cover and text design by Sandra Nobes
Cover images by Mic Looby
Set in 13 pt Bembo by Tou-Can Design
This book was printed in October 2012 at McPherson's Printing Group,
76 Nelson St, Maryborough, Victoria 3465, Australia
www.mcphersonsprinting.com.au

10 9 8 7 6 5 4 3 2 1

MIX
Paper from
responsible sources
FSC® C001695

The paper in this book is FSC® certified.
FSC® promotes environmentally responsible,
socially beneficial and economically viable
management of the world's forests.

Start here...

Everyone loves to laugh – children most of all. And every one of the jokes, riddles, rhymes and sayings in this book come from children just like you.

If you send me your favourite riddles and rhymes, the games you play and the jokes you tell, I might put them in another book. Email me at j.factor@unimelb.edu.au or write to me at the address below.

June Factor
PO Box 1063, Ivanhoe 3079

Not last night
but the night before,
Two tomcats came knocking
at my door.
I went to the door to Let them in,
And they knocked me out
with a rolling pin.

POSTMAN'S KNOCK

Knock knock.
Who's there?
One-eye.
One-eye who?
You're the one
I care for.

Knock knock.
Who's there?
Robin.
Robin who?
I'm Robin you, so hand over your money.

Knock knock.
Who's there?
Jump rope.
Jump rope who?
Just skip it.

Knock knock.
Who's there?
Ken.
Ken who?
Ken I give you some jellybeans?

Knock knock.
Who's there?
Amos.
Amos who?
A mosquito.

Knock knock.
Who's there?
Ana.
Ana who?
Another mosquito.

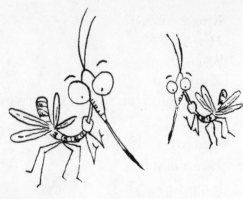

Knock knock.
Who's there?
Yeta.
Yeta who?
Yet another mosquito.

Knock knock.
Who's there?
Bear.
Bear who?
Bear bum.

Knock knock.
Who's there?
Nana.
Nana who?
Knock knock.
Who's there?
Nana.
Nana who?
Knock knock.
Who's there?
Aunt.
Aunt who?
Aunt you glad Nana's gone?

Knock knock.
Who's there?
Howard.
Howard who?
Howard I know?

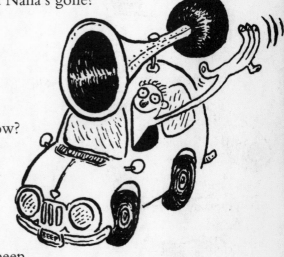

Knock knock.
Who's there?
Cargo.
Cargo who?
Car go beep beep.

Knock knock.
Who's there?
Mandy.
Mandy who?
Man de lifeboats, we are sinking!

Knock knock.
Who's there?
Mega.
Mega who?
Mega wish and blow out all the candles!

Knock knock.
Who's there?
Ivor.
Ivor who?
I've a sore hand from knocking on your door.

Knock knock.
Who's there?
Dewey.
Dewey who?
Dewey have to listen to all the knock-knock jokes?

I give away my first letter, I give away my second
letter, I give away all my letters. What am I?
A postman.

What starts with E and ends with E but has only
one letter in it?
An envelope.

He asked fair Ruth to marry him,
By letter she replied.
He read it, she refused him,
He shot himself and died.
He might have been alive now,
And she his happy bride,
If he had read the PS
Upon the other side.

I had written to Aunt Maud,
Who was on a trip abroad,
When I heard she'd died of cramp,
Just too late to save the stamp.

WAITING ROOM

Patient: I keep dreaming of a door with a sign
on it. I pull and I pull but the door
never opens.
Doctor: What does the sign say?
Patient: 'Push'.

Doctor, Doctor, I keep thinking I've lost my
memory.
When did this happen?
When did what happen?

Doctor, Doctor, I feel like a bee.
Well buzz off, I'm busy!

Doctor, Doctor, I keep thinking I'm a vampire.
Necks please!

Doctor, Doctor, I think I'm a bridge.
What's come over you?
Oh, two cars, a truck and a bus.

Doctor, Doctor, I must lose weight.
Diet, then.
But what colour?

Doctor, Doctor, I have a terrible cold!
Then you'd better avoid draughts.
All right, but can I play cards instead?

Doctor, Doctor, I keep thinking I'm a dog.
Take a seat. I'll be with you in a moment.
I'm sorry, I'm not allowed on the furniture.

Doctor, Doctor, I'm going to die in 59 seconds!
Wait a minute!

Nurse, please send in the second patient.
What's wrong with the first patient?
I don't know. That's why I'll start with the second.

Doctor: Why have you got a fish stuck in your ear?
Patient: It's my herring aid.

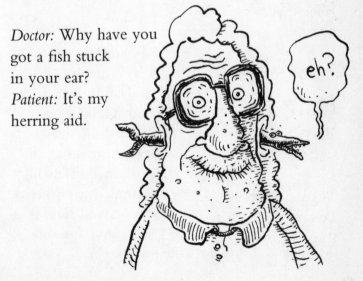

eh?

Found a peanut, found a peanut,
Found a peanut just now.
Found a peanut, found a peanut,
Found a peanut just now.

Been and ate it, been and ate it,
Been and ate it just now.
Been and ate it, been and ate it,
Been and ate it just now.

Other verses
Got a belly ache...
Saw the doctor...
Appendicitis...
Went to hospital...
Saw the surgeon...
Anaesthetic...
Cut me open...

Found the peanut...
Sewed me up again...
Lost the scissors...
Cut me open...
Found the scissors...
Sewed me up again...
Walked down the road...
Turned the corner...
What have I found?...
Found a peanut...

(to the tune of 'Oh my darling Clementine')

10

FACE IT

If all the boys ate fish and chips,
Wouldn't you have greasy lips?

Your eyes are like pedals – bicycle pedals.

What kind of ears do engines have?
Engineers.

How many ears did Daniel Boone have?
Three. A left ear, a right ear and a wild frontier.

What did one eye say to the other eye?
There's something between us and it smells.

Do you know the joke about the perfume?
I'd better not tell you – it stinks.

Up your nose with a rubber hose,
Twice as far with a chocolate bar,
Top that with a cricket bat!

DUNNIES AND DRAINS

How dry I am
How wet I'll be
If I can't find
The dunny key.

ABC
You smell like wee!

Roses die,
Violets wilt,
I hope you get covered in buckets of silt.

Baa baa black sheep,
Have you any cotton?
No sir, no sir,
It's all gone rotten.
None for the master,
None for the dame,
And none for the little boy
Who lives down the drain.

Fat and Skinny went to the zoo.
Fat got covered in elephant poo.
Skinny laughed to see such fun –
But Skinny trod in a sloppier one!

Fat and Skinny had a bath –
Fat farted and Skinny laughed.

TALL TALES

One day, the teacher told students to find out their families' favourite words.

When the boy got home, he asked his mum, who was busy cooking tea, 'What's your favourite word, Mum?'

'Shut up!'

So he wrote down 'Shut up'.

Then he asked his Dad, who was watching the footy (and his team was winning), 'What's your favourite word, Dad?'

'Yeah!'

So he wrote down 'Yeah'.

Then he went to his sister, who was singing 'Lollipop': 'What's your favourite word, Sis?'

'Lollipop a lollipop!'

So he wrote down 'Lollipop'.

Then he went to his little brother, who was watching the start of 'Batman': 'What's your favourite word, little brother?'

'Batman, Batman!'

So he wrote down 'Batman'.

Next day, the teacher asked him for his family's favourite words. So the boy said, 'Shut up!'

'Do you want to go to the principal?'

'Yeah!'

At the principal's office,
the principal said:
'What kind of punishment
do you deserve?'
'Lollipop a lollipop!'
'Who do you think you are?'
the principal said.
'Batman, Batman!'

Three men came to Australia, and they didn't
know any English.
The first man went to a singing class
and learnt how to say 'Mememememe'.
The second man went to a restaurant and learnt
how to say 'Fork and knife, fork and knife'.
The third man went to a lolly shop and learnt
how to say 'Goody goody gum drops'.
One day they all met on the street. Suddenly
they saw a dead man. A policeman came by
and said, 'Who killed this man?'
'Mememememe,' said the first man.
'How did you kill him?' asked the policeman.
'Fork and knife, fork and knife,' said the second
man.
Then the policeman shouted, 'OK, you're going
to jail right now!'
The third man said, 'Goody goody gum drops!'

One day there was a man walking down
the street.
He had two black stripes on his arm.
Another man asked him, 'Why are you walking
down the street with two black stripes?'
The man answered, 'Because my father died.'
The other man asked, 'Who was the other
person who died?'
'I rang up my brother, and his father died
as well.'

YUM YUM

Spaghetti on the plate
Spaghetti on the plate
Suck it up
Suck it up
Spaghetti on the plate.

Waiter, waiter, there's a fly in my soup.
Don't worry, the spider will eat it.

Waiter, waiter, give me a steak and make it lean.
Which way, sir?

Is there any soup
on the menu?
*There was, but
I wiped it off.*

Why did the
elephant sit on
the marshmallow?
*To keep from falling
in the cocoa.*

What kind of person loves cocoa?
A coconut.

What is the difference
between a monster
and a biscuit?
*You can't dip
a monster in your milk.*

What does a shark
eat with peanut butter?
Jellyfish.

Little Miss Muffet
Sat on her tuffet
Eating her curds and whey.
Along came a spider
And sat down beside her
And said, 'What's in the bowl, moll?'
'Curds, turd!'

Old Mother Hubbard
Went to the cupboard
To get the poor dog a bone.
When she got there
The cupboard was bare –
So they both starved to death.

WHO'S IN?

(counting-out rhyme)
Ink pink, you stink,
Ink onk, you ponk!

(skipping rhyme)
Over the garden wall
I let the baby fall.
My mother came and gave me a clout,
I asked her what she was shouting about.
She gave me another to match the others
Over the garden wall.

(clapping rhyme)
My mother, your mother, live down the street,
18, 19 Marble Street,
Every night they have a fight
And this is what they say all night:
Boys are rotten,
Made out of cotton,
Girls are sexy,
Made out of Pepsi,
Boys go to Jupiter
To get more stupider,
Girls go to Mars
To get more bras.
Incy wincy lollipop,
Incy wincy woo,
Incy wincy lollipop,
Boys love you
And that is true,
Bamboo!

(counting-out rhyme)
Ip dip dip,
Mickey Mouse in his house,
Pulling down his undies.
Quick, quick, smack his bum,
You're not it.

(counting-out rhyme)
Ip dip,
Sky blue.
Who's IT?
Not you.

(counting-out rhyme)
Redskin, you're in!
Boy scout, you're out!

HONEY HUSH,
DUNNY BRUSH

G I like you,
G I do,
G I hope you like me too.

I  U4URAQT

One, two, three-a-lairie
I saw Fred Astairie
Sitting on his you-
know-wherie
Kissing Ginger Rogers.

Oh how I love you,
honey hush,
Your hair looks like
a dunny brush,
Your lips are so pure,
They taste like manure,
Oh how I love you,
honey hush!

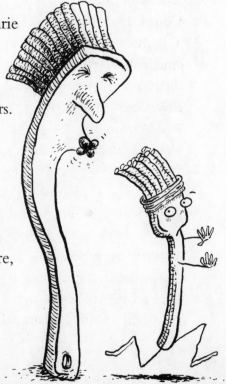

What do you call a girl who marries a hippy?
Mississippi.

Here comes the bride,
Big, fat and wide.
Here comes the groom,
As skinny as a broom.
Here comes the usher,
The old toilet flusher.

Roses are red
Violets are blue
The meat works stinks
And you do too.

Roses are white
Roses are red
You weigh more
Than ten tonnes of lead.

Little Miss Muffet
Sat on a tuffet
Writing her valentine.
Along came a spider
And sat down beside her
And said, 'Your legs are hairier than mine!'

COUNTING ON IT

How many balls of string would it take
to reach the moon?
One, but it would have to be a big one.

One two three,
Johnny caught a flea.
Flea died, Johnny cried,
One two three.

Three were in the parlour:
He, she and the lamp.
Two's company, three's a crowd –
That's why the lamp went out.

If two's company and three's a crowd,
what are four and five?
Nine.

What did the mathematician
say to the calculator?
I can count on you.

What did number 0 say
to number 8?
Nice belt.

What does one plus one equal?
Window.

What do two and two make?
A fish.

What do three and three make?
Eight.

What do four and four make?
A rocket.

If a butcher is 1.6 metres tall and wears
size 12 shoes, what does he weigh?
Meat.

CELEBRITY CORNER

Oh dearest Bess,
I like your dress.
Oh sweetest Liz,
I like your phiz.
Oh dearest Queen,
I've never seen
A face more like a soup tureen.

I'm Popeye the sailor man,
I live in a dunny can.
I eat all the flies
And spit out their eyes,
I'm Popeye the sailor man.

I'm Popeye the sailor man,
I live in a garbage can.
There's a hole in the middle
Where I do my piddle,
I'm Popeye the sailor man.

God save our gracious Queen,
Hit her on the head with a mandarine.

There was a cockatoo with two tags on its legs.
A man wanted to buy it. He asked the shop-
keeper what the cockatoo would do if he pulled
the left tag.
'He'll sing *God Save the Queen*,'
the shopkeeper said.
'And what will happen if I pull the right tag?'
'He'll sing *Advance Australia Fair*,'
said the shopkeeper.
'And what will happen if I pull both tags?'
Then the cockatoo spoke up and said,
'I'll fall off the perch!'

Little Jack Horner
Sat in the corner.
(His mum told him to because he was naughty.)

CLOCK WATCHERS

Early to bed,
Early to rise,
Makes you healthy,
Wealthy and wise.

Hickory dickory dock,
Two mice ran up the clock.
The clock struck one –
And the other received minor injuries.

I stood on the bridge at midnight
When a thought came into my head:
How silly of me to be standing here
When I ought to be home in bed.

Why did the girl sit on her watch?
Because she wanted to be on time.

What did the girl watch say to the boy watch?
Keep your hands to yourself.

An Aussie, an Englishman and a Frenchman
were walking in town when they came to a
tall building.

The Frenchman said, 'I bet I can drop my watch
from the top of that building, then run down and
catch it.'

The Frenchman raced to
the top of the building,
dropped his watch from the
highest window and raced
down again. He looked up,
but the watch wasn't there.
He looked down, and there
was his watch, smashed into
a thousand pieces.

Then the Englishman said,
'I'll do it.' He raced to the
top of the building, dropped his
watch from the highest window and raced down
again. He looked up, but the watch wasn't there.
He looked down, and there was his watch,
smashed into a thousand pieces.

Then the Aussie said, 'Now it's my turn.' He
raced to the top of the building, dropped his
watch from the highest window and raced down
again. He looked up, but the watch wasn't there.

He looked down, but it wasn't there either.
So he said, 'Let's go to the pub for an hour.'
So they did. When the drinking was over,
they went back to the building. The Aussie
looked up, but the watch wasn't there.
He looked down, but it wasn't there either.
So he said, 'Let's go to the cinema for an hour.'
So they did. When the film was over, they went
back to the building. The Aussie looked up –
and he was just in time to catch his watch.
The Englishman and the Frenchman were
amazed. They said, 'How did you manage to
catch it?' The Aussie said, 'It's two hours slow.'

MENAGERIE

A giraffe, an elephant, a camel, a bear, a pig,
a frog, two mice and a snake all sheltered under
one umbrella. How many got wet?
None. It wasn't raining.

What's yellow and black with red spots?
A leopard with the measles.

What's bright blue and weighs four tonnes?
An elephant holding its breath.

Mary had a little lamb,
She took it to a wedding.
Every time it made a sound,
She bashed its silly head in!

Mary had a little lamb,
Its fleece got full of fleas.
The shearers had to shear it off
And boy, did that lamb freeze!

Scritch
scritch

Why do giraffes
have long necks?
Because they have smelly feet.

Where was the rabbit
when the lights went out?
In the dark.

How do you catch a monkey?
*Hang upside down in a tree and
make banana noises.*

Why don't bananas
ever get lonely?
*Because they go around
in bunches.*

What do you get if you cross a centipede
with a parrot?
A walkie-talkie.

What's black and furry and moves on
sixteen wheels?
A skunk on skates.

What's white, furry and smells of peppermint?
A Polo bear.

When do elephants have eight feet?
When there are two of them.

What was the chicken doing on the runway?
Two kilometres an hour!

What's a frog's
favourite game?
Hopscotch.

POOCH & POODLE

There were two men in a pub. The first man had a dog.
The second man asked, 'Does your dog bite?'
'No,' said the first man.
So the second man patted the dog, and the dog bit him. He said, 'I thought your dog didn't bite?'
The first man said, 'It doesn't. This isn't my dog – I'm just minding it.'

What did the tree say to the dog?
I've got more bark than you.

What do you get if you cross a sheepdog with a flower?
A cauliflower.

A man was eating fish and chips in the street
when a woman walked past with a small dog.
The dog started yapping at the man's food.
'Can I throw him a bit?' asked the man.
'Of course,' said the woman.
So the man picked up the dog and threw it
over the wall.

What did the dog say when the farmer
pulled his tail?
'This is the end of me!'

Why do bulldogs have such flat noses?
Because they keep chasing parked cars.

What must you be careful not to do when it's
raining cats and dogs?
Step in a poodle.

NOEL NOEL

What do mice send each other at Christmas?
Christmouse cards.

What do monsters
sing at Christmas?
*Deck the halls with
poison ivy, falalalala,
lalalala.*

We had Granny
for Christmas last year.
Really? We had turkey.

What's Father Christmas's wife
called?
Mary.

What did Mrs Claus say to Santa Claus
when she saw clouds in the sky?
Looks like reindeer.

GREAT GAMES

Why wasn't Cinderella chosen for the softball team?
Because she ran away from the ball.

Why does it get hot after a football game?
Because all the fans leave.

The boy stood on the burning deck,
Playing a game of cricket,
The ball rolled up his trouser leg
And stumped the middle wicket.

TWAIN TWIPS

A cow was sitting on a railway track,
Her heart was all aflutter,
The train came roaring round the bend –
Crash! Bang!
Milk, meat, butter.

What is a twip?
*A twip is what a wabbit takes when it wides
on twains.*

NON-SENSE RIDDLES & GIGGLES

What's green, has four legs and can't fly?
A pool table.

Why are adults so boring?
Because they are all groan-ups.

How do you make a Venetian blind?
Poke it in the eye.

What disappears when
you stand up?
Your lap.

What do you call a farmer
who grows pickles?
The farmer in the dill.

What always succeeds?
A budgie without teeth.

What did the dirt say to the rain?
If this keeps up, my name will be mud.

How many hairs in a cat's tail?
None. They're all on the outside.

Where does the cook keep his pants?
In the pantry.

How do you make a tissue dance?
Put a little boogie in it.

Why are barbers always quick getting to work?
Because they know all the short cuts.

What did the wood say to the drill?
Go away, you bore me.

Why did the flea work overtime?
It was saving up to buy a dog.

What's better, a cow or a bull?
*A cow – a cow gives milk,
but a bull always charges.*

What's yellow and
wears a mask?
The lone lemon.

Why do heroes wear
big shoes?
Because of their amazing feats.

When is it all right
to drink from a saucer?
When you're a cat.

What is the best way
to make fire from two sticks?
*Make sure one of the sticks
is a match.*

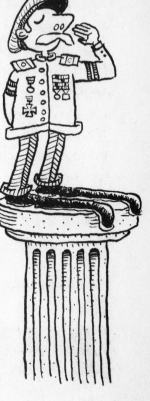

Why do skeletons hate winter?
*Because the cold goes
right through them.*

Why did the present surrender?
Because the wrapping paper had it surrounded.

What's smaller than an ant's pants?
A mozzie's cozzie.

What's smaller than a mozzie's cozzie?
A bee's knees.

What goes down a downpipe down and
up a downpipe down, but can't go
down a downpipe up or up a downpipe up?
An umbrella.

What did the priest say when there were
mosquitoes in church?
Let us spray.

What do you call a drunken ghost?
Methylated spirit.

What runs around a farm but never gets puffed?
The fence.

Why did the fly fly?
Because the spider spied 'er.

If your clothes were
stolen, what would
you go home in?
The dark.

What's pink and fluffy?
Pink fluff.

What do you call a man
with a shovel in his head?
Doug.

What do you call
a man without a shovel
in his head?
Douglas.

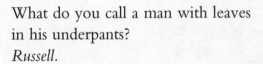

What do you call
a man with
a car on his head?
Jack.

What do you call a man with leaves
in his underpants?
Russell.

What do you call an elf who won't share?
Elfish.

Do you know the joke about the wall?
I'd better not tell you – you'd never get over it.

Do you know the joke about the limousine?
I'd better not tell you – it's too long.

What made the
Boy Scout dizzy?
Too many good turns.

What do you get when
two purple cars crash?
A violet crumble.

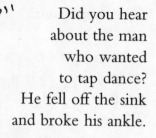

Did you hear
about the man
who wanted
to tap dance?
He fell off the sink
and broke his ankle.

Where do butchers dance?
At a meat ball.

What is as light as air but can't be held for long?
Your breath.

What do you sing on a snowman's birthday?
'Freeze a jolly good fellow…'.

What runs but never walks?
Water.

Why are there only eighteen letters
in the alphabet?
*Because ET went off in a UFO, and the CIA
went after him.*

BORN ON A TABLECLOTH

Mary had a little lamb,
She thought it was quite silly.
She threw it up into the air
And caught it by its —
Willie is a sheep dog
Sitting in the grass,
Up came a green ant
And bit him on the —
Ask no questions,
Tell no lies,
I saw a policeman
Doing up his —
Flies are annoying,
Spiders are worse,
And this is the end
Of my silly little verse.

Born on a tablecloth in Joe's Cafe,
Killed his mother in the USA,
Ran over his father with a double-decker bus
And killed his brother with Mortein Plus.
(to the tune of 'Davy Crockett')

(clapping rhyme)
Down down baby
Down down the roller-coaster
Sweet sweet baby
Sweet sweet don't let me go.
Gimme gimme cocopop
Gimme gimme rock
Gimme gimme cocopop
Gimme gimme rock.
I met a girlfriend
A trisket,
She said a crisket
A biscuit.
Ice-cream soda and vanilla on the top
Ice-cream soda and vanilla on the top.
Oh sheret walking down the street
Ten times a week –
I got it, I said it
I stole my mother's credit
I'm cool
I'm hot.
Punch me in the stomach
Three more times.
(punch your partner –
not too hard!)

Heigh ho, heigh ho,
It's off to work we go,
With a shovel and a spade
And a hand grenade,
Heigh ho, heigh ho, heigh ho,
heigh ho, heigh ho…
(to the tune of the Dwarves' song in Snow White*)*

Oh the sun shines down
On Charlie Chaplin.
His boots are cracklin'
For the want of blacknin'.
Oh the sun shines down
On Charlie Chaplin,
On Charlie Chaplin –
Hip hip hooray!
(to the tune of 'Oh the moon shines down')

Glory, glory, hallelujah,
Teacher hit me with a ruler.
The ruler broke in half,
We all began to laugh,
Glory, glory, hallelujah!

The bear climbed over the mountain,
The bear climbed over the mountain,
The bear climbed over the mountain,
And what do you think he saw?

He saw another mountain,
He saw another mountain,
He saw another mountain,
And what do you think he did?

The bear climbed over the mountain...
(and so on, and so on)

THIS TROUBLED LIFE

Never trouble trouble
Till trouble troubles you.
It only doubles trouble
And troubles others too.

Your life lies before you
Like a field of untrodden snow.
Be careful how you tread it,
For every step will show.

COMING TO A DEAD STOP

I went round a straight crooked corner
I saw a dead donkey die.

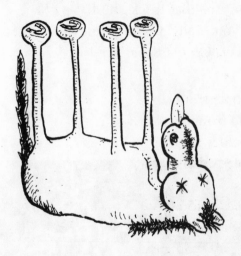

I went to stab him with my pistol,
But he sat up and kicked me in the eye.

Why do army officers wear boots
when they die?
*So they won't hurt their feet when they
'kick the bucket'.*

Oh Tom the toad, oh Tom the toad,
Why are you lying on the road?
You did not see that truck ahead,
And now you're lined with tyre tread.
(to the tune of 'Oh Christmas tree')

1st voice: Oh, you'll never get to heaven
2nd voice: Oh, you'll never get to heaven
1st voice: In a jumbo jet
2nd voice: In a jumbo jet
1st voice: 'Cos heaven ain't got
2nd voice: 'Cos heaven ain't got
1st voice: No runways yet!
2nd voice: No runways yet!

*(Each line in following verses
repeated in same way)*
Oh, you'll never get to heaven
In a biscuit tin
'Cos a biscuit tin
Has got biscuits in!

Oh, you'll never get to heaven
In a padded bra
'Cos a padded bra
Won't stretch that far!

Oh, you'll never get to heaven
On roller skates
'Cos you'll roll right past
Those pearly gates!

55

Knock knock.
Who's there?

Someone who can't reach the doorbell.

Hey diddle diddle
I've got a new riddle

so turn the page ...

ALIENS

What did the alien say to the petrol pump?
Why have you got your finger stuck in your ear?

When you run into a three-headed alien,
what should you say?
Goodbye, goodbye, goodbye!

What is an alien's normal eyesight?
20-20-20.

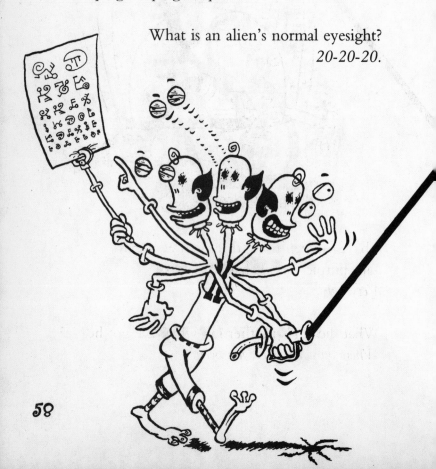

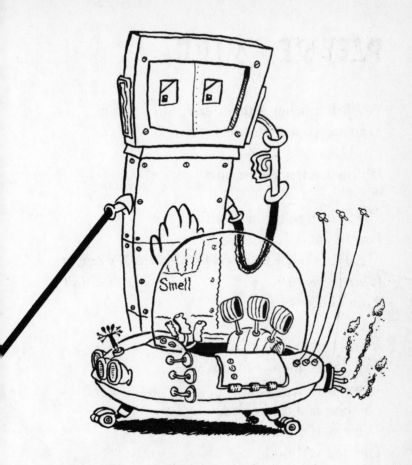

I have a green nose, three red eyes and
four purple ears. What am I?
Very ugly.

What did ET's mother say when ET got home?
Where on earth have you been?

PLEASE, MISS

Teacher, teacher, I don't care,
I can see your underwear.
It is black, it is white,
Oh my lord, it's dynamite!

Miss, can I go to the toilet?
First I want to hear your ABC.
ABCDEFGHIJKLMNOQRSTUVWXYZ.
Where is your P?
Running down my pants.

A boy said to a girl named Jenny,
'My dog is good at maths.'
'Show me,' said Jenny.
The boy said to the dog,
'What is 100 minus 100?'
The dog said nothing.

Would you like a pocket calculator, sir?
No thanks, I know how many pockets I've got.

What is a very hard subject?
The study of rocks.

School's out, school's out,
Teacher wore her bloomers out!

How do dinosaurs pass their exams?
With extinction.

No more pencils, no more books,
No more teachers' dirty looks;
When the teacher rings the bell
Grab your bag and run like hell!

Teacher: Simon, can you say your name
backwards?
Simon: No, mis'.

Why did the computer cross the road?
Because the chicken programmed it.

Who is a monkey's favourite teacher?
The teacher who goes bananas.

When you're young, your parents teach you
to walk and talk.
When you're older, they tell you to sit down
and shut up.

Why did the jellybeans go to school?
They wanted to be smarties.

DO-IT-YOURSELF

BOOKSHELF

Don't Wake the Baby — ELSIE CRIES

Yellow Stream — I.P. Daily

FIRST PRIZE — Hedda de Class

Catastrophe in the Cow Shed — O.O. Flung Dung

Peas & Broccoli — E. Tittup

KNICKERS ON THE LINE

What did the hat say to the scarf?
You hang around while
I go on ahead.

Did you hear about the
robbery at the laundry?
Two pegs held up a skirt.

My father was a sailor
At the battle of Waterloo.
The wind blew up his trousers
And he didn't know what to do.

Mrs Brown went to town
With her knickers hanging down.

What's the time?
Half past nine.
Hang your knickers on the line.
If they tear, I don't care,
Go and buy another pair.

What's the time?
Ten to nine.
Hang your knickers on the line.
When they're dry
Bring them in,
Put them in the biscuit tin.
Eat a biscuit, eat a cake,
Eat your knickers by mistake!

Old Dan Tucker was a good old man.
He washed his face in a frying pan.
He combed his hair with a wagon wheel
And died with a toothache in his heel.

When you get old
and cannot see
Put on your specs
and think of me.

Knock, knock.
Who's there?
Disco.
Disco who?
Dis coat's too
big for me.

DOCTORS AND NURSES

Knock, knock.
Who's there?
Arch.
Arch who?
Bless you!

Which travels faster, heat or cold?
Heat. You can catch a cold.

What bone likes to
rock and roll?
A hip bone.

What bone
appreciates a joke?
A funny bone.

What colour is a hiccup?
Burple.

My father came from China,
My father came from France,
And I came from hospital
Without my underpants!

Happy birthday to you.
Stick your head down the loo...
Taste it, don't waste it!
Happy birthday to you.

Why did the toilet paper roll down the hill?
Because it wanted to get to the bottom.

What did one lift say to the other lift?
I think I'm coming down with something.

Nurse: How is the girl who swallowed
the dollar, Doctor?
Doctor: No change yet!

Doctor: Did you drink orange juice after your
bath?
Patient: After drinking the bath water I didn't
have much room for the orange juice.

Doctor, doctor, will you help me out?
Certainly, which way did you come in?

Did you hear the one about the germ?
No.
Never mind, I don't want it to spread.

Doctor: Yes, what is it?
Patient: Will this cream you gave me clear up
the red spots on my body?
Doctor: I never make rash promises.

BLOOD AND GUTS

What star goes to jail?
A shooting star.

What part of a window
hurts?
A window pane.

A man sat down by a sewer
And by the sewer he died.
When the case was brought
to the coroner's court,
They called it sewer-cide.

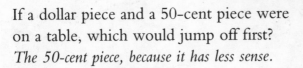

If a dollar piece and a 50-cent piece were
on a table, which would jump off first?
The 50-cent piece, because it has less sense.

Knock, knock.
Who's there?
Icecream.
Icecream who?
I scream when I see a monster.

(To the tune of 'John Brown's Body')
There was a paratrooper in the 48th brigade,
There was a paratrooper in the 48th brigade,
There was a paratrooper in the 48th brigade,
And he ain't going to jump no more!

Chorus
Glory, glory what a hell of a way to go, hey!
Glory, glory what a hell of a way to go, hey!
Glory, glory what a hell of a way to go—
And he ain't going to jump no more!

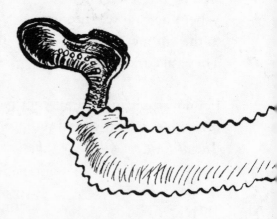

(Verses—repeat each line three times, then add:
'And he ain't going to jump no more')
The Sergeant said, 'It's easy—
when you jump you pull the cord'...

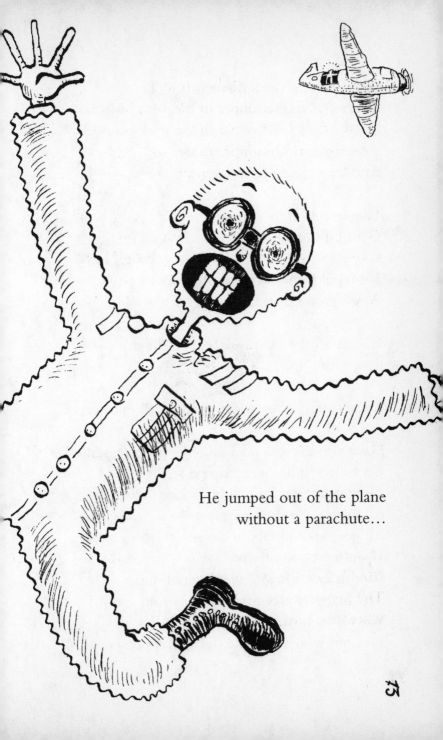

He jumped out of the plane
without a parachute...

He landed on the target like a blob
of strawberry jam...

They scraped him off the target
with a piece of masonite...

They put him in a jar and
sent him home to his mum...

They put him on the mantelpiece
for everyone to see...

He fell off the mantelpiece, and the cat
licked him up...

(*Final chorus*: Glory, glory what a hell of a way...)

Have you ever wondered as the hearse goes by
If you might be the next one to die?
They wrap you up in a big white sheet
And drop you down six feet.
All goes well for about a week,
Then the coffin starts to leak.
Worms crawl in and grubs crawl out
And maggots play pingpong on your snout.
Your liver turns a sickly green
And out comes pus like thick whipped cream.

Jingle bells, jingle bells,
Santa Claus is dead.
GI Joe, GI Joe,
Shot him in the head.
Barbie doll, Barbie doll,
Tried to save his life.
Teddy bear, teddy bear,
Stabbed her with his knife.

Jingle bells, jingle bells,
Santa Claus is dead.
Rudolph got a .44
And shot him in the head.
Jolly, jolly Mrs Claus
Tried to save his life.
But Barbie doll didn't know
And stabbed him with a knife.

Roses are red
Violets are blue,
You might think it's funny
But I just spew.

TRAFFIC JAM

When do you get that rundown feeling?
When a car hits you.

Mary had a little lamb,
'Twas awful dumb, it's true;
It followed her in a traffic jam
And now it's mutton stew.

Little dog
Busy street
Car comes
Sausage meat.

Why do people fly to Hawaii for a holiday?
Because it's too far to walk.

Why did the man sleep under the car?
He wanted to wake up oily in the morning.

What bird is like a car?
A goose, because it honks.

When is a car not a car?
When it turns into a driveway.

Yesterday my cousin Jane
Said she was an aeroplane
But I wanted
further proof
So I pushed her
off the roof.

A man stood on the
railway line,
He heard the
engine squeal.
The guard took out
his little spade
And scraped him
off the wheel.

What has four
wheels and flies?
A garbage truck.

MOGGIES AND DOGGIES

What goes tick tick, woof woof?
A watchdog.

What do you get when
you cross a dog with a lion?
A terrified postman.

Roses are red
Violets are blue,
The bulldog next door
Reminds me of you.

What do you get when you cross a dog
and an egg?
Pooched eggs.

Why do dogs scratch themselves?
*Because they are the only ones who know
where it itches.*

I wish I had some bricks
To build the chimney higher,
To stop that blasted tomcat
From putting out the fire.

What kind of dog does
Count Dracula like?
A bloodhound.

What did the two seasick dogs say?
Ruff, ruff!

I once had a dog
Without any sense,
He ran round the house
And barked at the fence.

What do you call a wet pup?
A soggy doggy.

If a fat cat is a flabby tabby, what is
a very small cat?
An itty bitty kitty.

You're a dog!
Thank you for the compliment.
Dogs bark, bark is on trees,
trees are part of nature, and
nature is beautiful.

There were ten cats on a boat
and one jumped out.
How many were left?
None. They were all copycats.

COCKADOODLEMOO

Why do baby ducks walk softly?
Cos' little baby ducks can't walk hardly.

What do you get when you put
four ducks in a box?
A box of quackers.

A paralysed donkey passing by
Kicked a blind man in the eye.
'Oh,' said the blind man, 'that's not fair.'
'Oh,' said the donkey, 'I don't care.'

We sat in the greenest fields,
The greenest fields we could find,
But Nathan sat in something else
The cows had left behind.

What did the city dude say when
he found a milk carton in the grass?
'Hey, I found a cow's nest!'

How does a pig get to hospital?
In a hambulance.

What do you get when you cross a cow
and a rooster?
A cockadoodlemoo.

Cat's got the measles, dog's got the flu,
Donkey's got the chicken pox, and so have you.

Roses are red
Violets are blue.
My pigs smell
Just like you.

Mary had a little lamb
She taught it how to sing,
But now it is an old ram
You ought to hear the thing!

JUNGLY JOKES

What's brown, has a big tail, lives in Australia and ticks?
A kangaroo with a watch in his pocket.

What kind of key cannot open a door?
A monkey.

What do you get when you cross a crocodile with a rose?
I don't know, but I wouldn't try smelling one.

What is a crocodile's favourite card game?
Snap.

Roses are red
Violets are blue,
You look like a monkey
So go back to the zoo.

What do you call a camel with three humps?
Humphrey.

What do you call a camel with no humps?
Hump-free.

What's yellow and smells like bananas?
Monkey vomit.

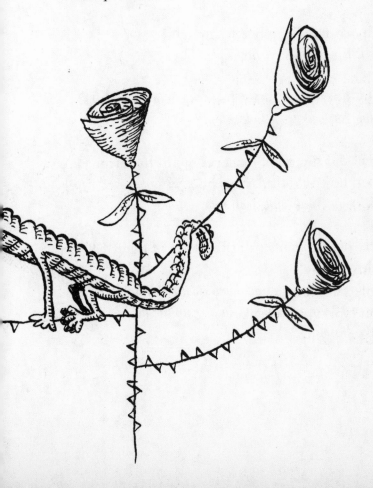

How do you catch a squirrel?
Act like a nut.

What is the largest mouse in the world?
A hippopotamouse.

What is grey, has four legs, big ears and a trunk?
A mouse going on holidays.

Why couldn't the bee fly straight?
He left his specks on the wall.

Why does an elephant have so many wrinkles?
Have you ever tried to iron one?

What did the hotel manager say to the elephant
when he couldn't pay his bill?
Pack your trunk and clear out.

Why do elephants paint the soles of their feet
yellow?
*So they can hide upside down in the custard. Have
you ever seen an elephant hiding upside down
in the custard?*
No.
Shows what a good disguise it is.

Why are skunks so smart?
They have lots of scents.

What do you get if you cross a giant gorilla with
a skunk?
King Pong.

What's white and fluffy and swings through
the jungle?
A meringue-utan.

CAST-A-NET

Why can't two elephants go swimming
at the same time?
They only have one pair of trunks.

Why was the crab sent to prison?
Because he kept pinching things.

What's the best way to
communicate with a fish?
Drop a line.

What's yellow, black
and dangerous?
Shark-infested custard.

What is full of holes
and still holds water?
A sponge.

Which musical instrument could be used for
fishing?
Castanets.

What did the tide say to the beach as it came in?
Nothing. It waved.

What did the tide say to the beach as it came in?
Long time no sea.

What do sea monsters eat?
Fish and ships.

What goes 'Ouch, ouch,
ouch, ouch, ouch,
ouch, ouch, *ouch*'?
An octopus with tight shoes.

What did Cinderella wear to the beach?
Glass flippers.

PIE IN THE SKY

What pie can fly?
A magpie.

Why did the man cross the road?
Because he thought he was a chicken.

Why did the chicken cross the playground?
To get to the other slide.

Why did the bubble-gum cross the road?
Because it was stuck to the chicken's foot.

What has webbed feet and fangs?
Count Duckula.

What is a chicken's favourite vegetable?
Eggplant.

What's the best grade you can get
at chicken school?
Egg-cellent.

Joe: I once had a parrot
for five years and it never
said a word.
Bill: It must have been
tongue-tied.
Joe: No, it was stuffed.

On top of Mount Snowy
All covered with grass
I shot a poor eagle
Right up his...
Now don't be mistaken
Don't be misled
I shot the poor eagle
Right up his leg.

Hickory dickory dock,
The mouse ran up the clock.
From deep inside a cuckoo cried,
'At least you ought to knock.'

What's black, white and dangerous?
A magpie with a machine gun.

Red, white and blue
Dirty cockatoo,
Sitting on a lamp post
Telling you what to do.

If your peacock lays an egg in your neighbour's garden, who would own the egg?
Nobody. Peacocks can't lay eggs, only peahens can.

How did the tired sparrow land?
By sparrowchute.

WABBITS IN THE WEFWIGEWATOR

When is it proper to drink
rabbits' milk?
When you are a baby rabbit.

Where do you find rabbits?
It depends where they were lost.

Why was the rabbit in the
Westinghouse refrigerator?
He was westing.

How do you know
when you have 200 rabbits in your refrigerator?
When the door won't shut.

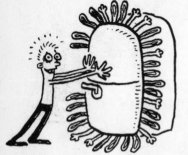

How do you know when
you have 200 rabbits in
your refrigerator?
When your fridge is hopping!

Are carrots good for your eyes?
Sure — ever seen a rabbit with glasses?

Why didn't Joe put an
advertisement in the paper
when he lost his rabbit?
Joe's rabbit never reads the paper.

What should you do with a rabbit
who is eating a dictionary?
Take the words right out of his mouth.

What did the bridegroom give his rabbit bride?
An 18-carrot gold ring.

What do you get if you cross a rabbit and
a garden hose?
Hare spray.

How do you catch a rabbit?
*You hide behind a tree and
make a noise like a carrot.*

What did the rabbit say to the carrot?
It's been nice gnawing you.

WIGGLE YOUR HIPS

Keep smiling. It makes everyone
wonder what you're up to.

Forget me not
Forget me never
And you will have
A friend for ever.

(skipping rhyme)
Little Sally Warner
Sitting in a corner
Rise, Sally, rise!
Wipe your weepin' eyes
Wiggle your hips
Let your backside slip.

A heart is not a plaything,
A heart is not a toy,
But if you want it broken
Just give it to a boy.

(skipping rhyme)
When will you get married
1, 2, 3 (etc.)
How many children will you have?
1, 2, 3 (etc.)
What will you live in?
House, mansion, shack.
What will you drive?
Ford, Holden, wreck.
Will you get divorced?
Yes, no, yes, no (etc.)

Love many, trust a few
But always paddle your own canoe.

(skipping rhyme)
Bread and butter, marmalade, jam
Who do you think is [*name*]'s boyfriend?
A, B, C, D…David.
David, David, come to tea
David, David, marry me.
Yes, no, yes, no…
Where will we get married?
Church, bedroom, bathroom, hall…
What will I wear?
Silk dress, bikini, underwear, nothing…
What will David wear?
Nice suit, boardshorts, underwear, nothing…
How many babies will we have?
1, 2, 3, 4, 5…
How many bottles will we need?
1, 2, 3, 4, 5…
How many nappies will we need?
1, 2, 3, 4, 5…

(skipping rhyme)
Turn to the east
Turn to the west
Turn to the one
That you like the best.

Shirley Temple is a star
S-T-A-R.
She can do the curtsey
She can do the Twist
She can do anything, just like this.

What kind of table should you be able
to swim in?
A pool table.

THE BANKS OF THE HANKEY PANKEY

(clapping rhyme)
Ronald McDonald [*clap twice*] Fucheeka
Ronald McDonald [*clap twice*] Fucheeka
Ah shoo shoo wah wah Fucheeka
I've got a boyfriend Fucheeka
He's so cute Fucheeka
Sweet cherry on the top, plop [*thumbs up*]
Icecream soda on the bottom floor drop
[*thumbs down*].

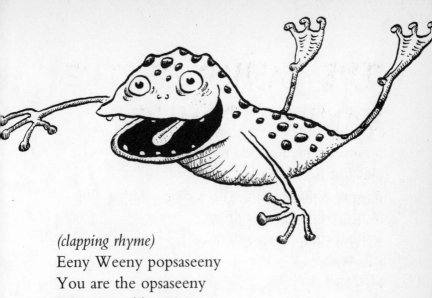

(clapping rhyme)
Eeny Weeny popsaseeny
You are the opsaseeny
Education, liberation
I like you.
Down, down baby
Down by the rollercoaster,
Sweet, sweet baby
I love you.
Caught you with your boyfriend
In this place,
Down by the banks of the Hankey Pankey
the bullfrog jumps from bank to banky
With an eep ipe opey dopey
And an eep ipe opey dopey yeah!

(clapping rhyme)
Hey [*name*]
I think I hear my name.
Hey [*name*], there it goes again.
You're wanted on the telphone
But if it isn't [*name*]
You're not at home, with a ring a ding a ding
With a ring a ding a ding
With a ring a ding a ding
Oh yeah
Oh yeah.

(clapping rhyme)
Dagwood and Blondie went to town
Blondie wore a dressing gown
Dagwood bought the evening paper
And this is what it said:
'Close your eyes and count to ten
And if you can, go to the end.'
1, 2, 3, 4, 5, 6, 7, 8, 9, 10.

EATING BREAD
WITH FROGS ON

Back to you with knobs on
Eating bread with frogs on
Walking round with clogs on
Neh neh neh neh neh.

Is it good manners to eat fried chicken with
your fingers?
No. You should eat your fingers separately.

Which hand should you use to stir tea?
Neither. It is better to use a spoon.

Why are cooks cruel?
Because they beat eggs,
whip cream and
batter fish.

Roses are red
Violets are blue,
Lemons are sour
And so are you.

My mother came from Cuba and my father
came from Iceland.
Does that mean you're an ice cube?

What do you get if you cross a refrigerator
and a radio?
Cool music.

What do you serve but never eat?
Tennis balls.

Waiter, waiter, there's a button in my salad.
It must have fallen in while the salad was dressing,
madam.

Waiter, waiter, what's this in my soup?
I've no idea, sir — all insects look the same to me.

The cannibal wedding was going fine
until someone toasted the bride.

What did the monster eat after he had his teeth
pulled out?
The dentist.

What sort of jam shouldn't you eat?
A traffic jam.

What do polar bears eat for lunch?
Ice burgers.

What do you call a spider that eats a lot?
A wider spider.

JELLY CAKES AND BELLY ACHES

What did the chocolate bar say to the lollipop?
Hullo, sucker.

What nut has no shell?
A doughnut.

As I went up the silver lake
I met a little rattlesnake
He ate so much of jelly cake
It made his little belly ache.

Little boy
Green plum
One gulp
Aching tum.

Australian people are so sexy
This is how they drink their Pepsi:
Slurp, slurp and then a little burp.

What are hundred and thousands?
Smartie poo.

PJs AND TOOTHPASTE

What do you give an elephant who is exhausted?
Trunkquillisers.

What's a bull called when it goes to sleep?
A bulldozer.

What do you get when you cross two banana peels?
A pair of slippers.

What tuba can't play?
A tuba toothpaste.

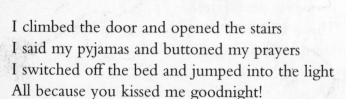

Her teeth are like stars,
They come out at night.

I climbed the door and opened the stairs
I said my pyjamas and buttoned my prayers
I switched off the bed and jumped into the light
All because you kissed me goodnight!

He stood on the bridge at midnight
Interrupting my sweet repose,
He was a giant mosquito
The bridge was the bridge of my nose.

Now that we've reached the end,
why don't you make like a tree
and leave?

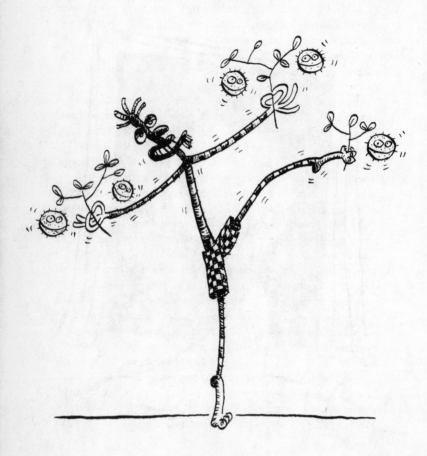

For Adults

I have been compiling collections of Australian children's playground rhymes, riddles and jokes since 1983. The popularity of these books suggests that both children and adults take pleasure in collections of children's verbal lore: the playful traditions of childhood bind us across countless generations.

Primary school-age children are the principal inheritors, adaptors and innovators of the material in these collections. At this period in their lives, they are comparatively small, weak, ignorant and powerless. They are also endlessly curious and imaginative. Play, including play with language, is the medium through which children extend their knowledge and their control of the world around them. In play, children are the initiators, the rule-makers and the participants. This is an arena, whether of words or games, in which direction and control belong not to adults but to children. Here they are powerful.

Youngsters mimic parents, teachers, doctors, politicians – the authorities – in order to mock them. Humour is a constant, often expressed through pun and parody. No subject is sacrosanct, no words forbidden. While I have chosen not to include in these collections material from the large opus of obscene and abusive children's lore, it is essential for adults genuinely interested in the reality of child life – as distinct from its romantic image – to recognise the importance such material plays in children's lives. Vulgarity and an array of abusive expressions replicate the patterns and values of adult culture; they are also ways in which the young can appear 'grown-up'.

Readers who are interested in exploring this subject and/ or contributing further examples of children's verbal lore are welcome to contact me at the Australian Centre, University of Melbourne, Vic. 3010 (j.factor@unimelb.edu.au)

June Factor was born in Poland and grew up in Australia, where she has been writing books and articles for a long time. She has a special interest in what children do when they are playing. That's why she has collected many of the rhymes, riddles, jokes and sayings that children use in their play and friendships. As everyone was once a child, this oral literature belongs to us all, but especially to children whose pleasure it is to play with words and ideas.

Mic Looby was born, after years of non-existence, in 1969 in Windsor, New South Wales. After doodling his way through school in Canberra and Melbourne, he accidentally earned a degree in journalism and went on to work as newspaper writer/cartoonist/illustrator in Australia and Hong Kong. Now he is a writer, editor and freelance illustrator.